À Hélène, la femme de ma vie,
qui n'a maintenant plus peur des araignées (enfin presque).
—G. B.

Many thanks to Dr. Tom Walla, Assistant Professor of Biology at Mesa State College,
for his considerable contributions to this book.

Published in North America in 2007 by Two-Can Publishing
11571 K-Tel Drive
Minnetonka, MN 55343
www.two-canpublishing.com

First published in France under the title *Les sales bêtes: ni sales, ni bêtes.*
English text copyright © 2007 by Two-Can Publishing.
Copyright © 2006 by Éditions Milan—300, rue Léon Joulin—31101 Toulouse Cedex 9—France
www.editionsmilan.com

Library of Congress Cataloging-in-Publication Data
Bonotaux, Gilles, 1956-
[Sales bêtes. English]
Dirty rotten bugs? : arthropods unite to tell their side of the story / written and illustrated by Gilles Bonotaux.
p. cm.
Summary: "Insects, arachnids, centipedes, and millipedes speak out against their reputation
as dirty rotten bugs and explain why they deserve respect from humans"—Provided by publisher.
ISBN 978-1-58728-593-6 (hardcover)
1. Arthropoda—Juvenile literature. I. Title.
QL434.15.B6613 2007
595--dc22   2006038

1 2 3 4 5 / 11 10 09 08 07
Printed in Singapore

DIRTY ROTTEN BUGS?

Arthropods Unite to Tell Their Side of the Story

written and illustrated by GILLES BONOTAUX

Minnetonka, Minnesota

My fellow arthropods—insects, spiders, centipedes, millipedes...you know who you are—it's time for us to stand united! We've been called "dirty rotten bugs" long enough. Let's tell these simple-minded humans that they are not all-powerful on this planet. Let's show them who we really are, and why we deserve their respect. Together we are strong!

Right on!

Definitely!

You said it!

6

An **arthropod** is an invertebrate animal, which means we don't have a spine. (But watch out, we aren't spineless cowards!) Arthropods have an outer skeleton called an **exoskeleton,** a body that's divided into sections, and jointed legs.

| Arthropod: Skeleton outside | Human: Skeleton inside | Slug: No skeleton at all |

Hey junior! The table on the next page shows how scientists organize the main kinds of arthropods (technically called the Arthropoda phylum) on the tree of life.

Louse Power

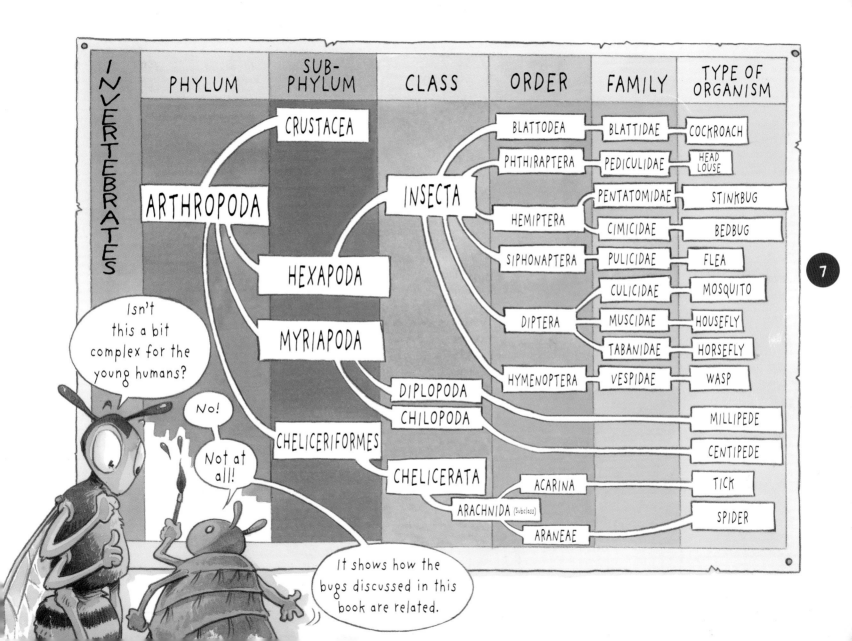

FOUR CLASSES OF ARTHROPODS

Out of the classes of arthropods, there are four that seem to bother you humans the most. Others, like Crustacea (shellfish), seem to have won you over, so we aren't going to talk about those guys here.

Chelicerata (kuh-liss-uh-RA-tuh): Invertebrate arthropods with eight jointed legs. Arachnids—spiders, scorpions, and ticks—are the main members of this group. They have no jaws or antennae, but they do have chelicerae (two fanglike, venomous mouthparts).

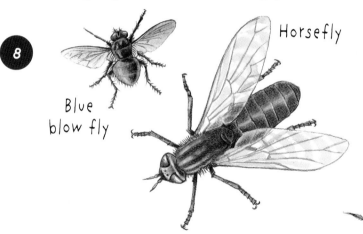

Horsefly

Blue blow fly

House spider

Tick

Scorpion

Insecta: Invertebrate arthropods with six jointed legs. As the name suggests, these are the insects: ants, bees, butterflies, beetles, grasshoppers, and flies. An insect's body is divided into three segments: head, thorax, and abdomen. Insects have three pairs of legs and two antennae. Most insects have wings, though they may be very small or completely useless.

Diplopoda and **Chilopoda:** Diplopoda (millipedes) and Chilopoda (centipedes) are invertebrate arthropods with many jointed legs. Like insects, they have a pair of antennae and grinding jaws called **mandibles.** They breathe through many small tiny holes on their bodies called spiracles. But unlike insects, their bodies are divided into many segments, each of which has one or two pairs of legs. They have lots of legs, but not 1,000, as many people think!

Millipede

COCKROACHES

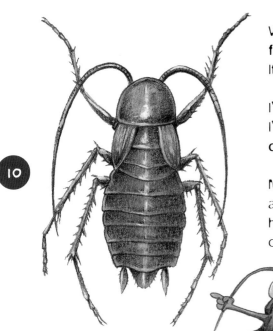

We're usually called cockroaches, but, in fact, we are part of the Blattidae family—the blattids for short! We are a common sight to humans in cities. It's a good thing we can run fast!

I'm the **Oriental cockroach** (*Blatta orientalis*). In fact, I'm the true cockroach. I'm 20 to 25 millimeters (0.8 to 1 in) long and dark colored. My female companion is nearly **apterous.** That means she has practically no wings.

My friend the **American cockroach** (*Periplaneta americana*) is a strong guy, also known as *Blattella americana*. It lives mainly on boats and sometimes in harbors, but finds it difficult to get used to houses. Must be the call of the open sea!

The **German cockroach** (*Blattella germanica*) is lighter in color. Its wings are longer than its body. It likes to make itself at home where you do.

Oriental cockroach
(*Blatta orientalis*)
Blattidae family
Blattodea order
Insecta class

10

Hello!

Guten Tag!

We also have some cousins in the countryside, but they don't bother you humans much. Some, like the wood cockroach, live in the forest, while others live under stones.

More than 2,500 species of cockroaches share the planet. We are found mainly in tropical countries. We even have an Australian cousin, the giant burrowing cockroach (*Macropanesthia rhinoceros*), that weighs more than 30 grams (1 oz). Better be friends with him!

Maybe you've noticed that we cockroaches go out mainly at night and hide during the day. Let's try an experiment.

Got it? Cockroaches hate light. We are **lucifugal**.

We're also some of the fastest insects in the world.

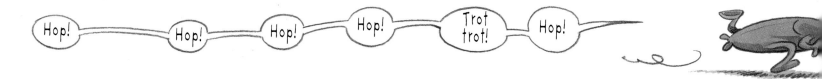

We like it when it's warm, because we're tropical creatures. This is why we like your homes—the temperature is just right. We eat everything. You could say we're **omnivores,** like you!

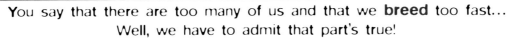

You say that there are too many of us and that we **breed** too fast... Well, we have to admit that part's true!

Each female cockroach can lay 6 to 50 eggs. Until they hatch, the eggs are kept in a kind of pouch (ootheca) that the female carries on her abdomen. Well protected in the ootheca, the future baby cockroaches have a better chance of surviving.

The newborn blattids (the larvae) already look a lot like their parents, but smaller and without wings. Childhood doesn't last long....The little cockroaches will soon become adults.

You also say we are creepy looking. Maybe from a human point of view. We could say the same about you! Have you taken a good look at yourselves?

Enough is enough! What have you got against us? You say that we are dirty and that we carry diseases. But that's simply not true! We are harmless and clean. If you want us to go away, don't leave food lying around and sweep the floor every day. Oh, and one more thing: don't heat your home—even in winter.

MILLIPEDES

We left with 500 of us, but with swift reinforcement, 5,000 of us arrived at our destination.

Wait! Is that a bird?

YIKES!

I feel like curling up into a ball!

Millipedes are peaceful and shy creatures. We are saprophagous, which means that we feed on decaying organic matter. Our only means of defense is to curl up into a ball and play dead.

14

As **diplopods,** we have two pairs of legs per segment. They don't help us run very fast, but we can walk in a straight line.

4 legs per segment

side view

underneath view

Oh when the millipedes... go marching in... oh when the millipedes go marching in...

We feel less nervous in groups!

Millipede
Julidae family
Diplopoda class
Myriapoda subphylum
Arthropoda phylum

Why are we considered dirty rotten bugs? Some of us produce a stinky, smelly substance that can be dangerous to humans. But the main reason is because we have been known (very rarely—relax!) to invade a whole area: houses, railroad tracks, roads. Thousands of us milling about everywhere! Why? Not even your experts know much about it, and neither do we. And if we did know, we wouldn't tell you!

CENTIPEDES

WE BITE

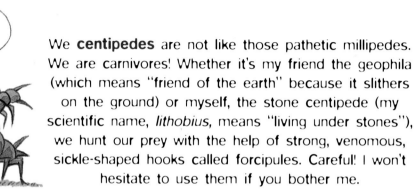
Hey old man! You're ugly!

Look who's talking!

We **centipedes** are not like those pathetic millipedes. We are carnivores! Whether it's my friend the geophila (which means "friend of the earth" because it slithers on the ground) or myself, the stone centipede (my scientific name, *lithobius*, means "living under stones"), we hunt our prey with the help of strong, venomous, sickle-shaped hooks called forcipules. Careful! I won't hesitate to use them if you bother me.

two legs per segment

head with forcipules

While diplopods like the millipede walk straight, a **chilopod's** walk has a wavelike, side-to-side motion. This is because we have just one pair of legs per segment.

Stone centipede
(Lithobius)
Chilopoda class
Myriapoda subphylum
Arthropoda phylum

Hey, can you do this?

WASPS

WE STING

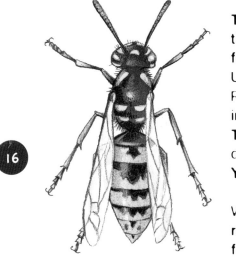

The sun just came up, and it's breakfast time. It could have been a beautiful day for you humans to enjoy the outdoors. Unfortunately, here come the **wasps!** Ruined picnics? That's us! Making irritated grown-ups shake their napkins? That's us! Forcing you to keep food and drinks covered? Stinging small children? Yes, that's us again!

We wasps, fierce and brave, are ready to risk our lives for a few crumbs of cake, an ounce of jam, or a sip of soda!

Common wasp
(*Vespula vulgaris*)
Vespidae family
Hymenoptera order
Insecta class

With a big apple pie!

Air base? Humans detected down there!

ATTACK!

Here's some good advice: go home and leave the grub for us!

Hey, Boss, we really are dirty rotten bugs!

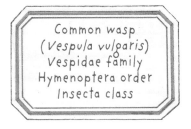

Getting mad at us won't help! That annoys us even more, and we would then be forced to sting you.

Do not confuse us with honeybees, whose sweet labors you shamelessly steal. While they are part of the Hymenoptera order like we are, honeybees have stockier bodies. And after they sting, they die. We don't!

Honeybees
The hooklike stinger gets stuck in the skin. The bee can't get away without losing part of its body—and its life!

Other bees and wasps
We sting, fly away, and are ready to start all over again.

My friend the **ant** also belongs to the Hymenoptera order. Bees, ants, and wasps have one thing in common: our children (larvae) cannot survive on their own. Like bees and ants, we wasps live in colonies and work together to care for the next generation.

The end of summer is mating season for us wasps. After mating, the fertilized females (called queens) hibernate over the winter. Then, in spring, each female starts building a nest to lay eggs and raise a brood of workers. As soon as these young wasps reach maturity, they start doing jobs for her: making the nest, preparing compartments called cells where the eggs will be laid, and feeding the next generation of larvae. The queen can then focus on her job: laying eggs.

A wasp's nest is basically a cluster of cells. The whole thing is surrounded by a papery membrane or "envelope" made of chewed-up wood fibers.

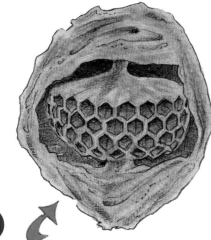

18

yellow jacket
nest

paper wasp
nest

When winter comes, everyone dies except the fertilized females, who form new colonies the following year. It's tough being a wasp!

The **common wasp,** or **yellow jacket,** nests in stone walls or attics. Our cousins the hornets do, too.

The **Germanic wasp** prefers abandoned burrows. **Polistine wasps,** also known as **paper wasps,** build very small nests on plant stems.

To be or not to be?

Now that you know the difference between a wasp and a bee, can you tell a common wasp from a paper wasp, a German wasp from a **bee wolf?** To do so, take a close look at our abdomens in the drawings below. But watch out, you might get stung!

Common wasp

Germanic wasp

Paper wasp

Bee wolf (philanthus)

Hornet

Zebra?

You don't belong here. Scram!

The French have a saying, *se mettre dans un guêpier* ("to put yourself in a wasp's nest"), which means to find yourself in trouble. Hope this doesn't happen to you!

Wasps have such narrow waists that a lot of women envy us. To be able to claim a "**wasp waist,**" your ancestors wore tight corsets that slimmed their silhouettes.

Ridiculous!

Walking alone?

That's not safe!

Nice pollen!

HORSEFLIES

WE BITE

She's the biter, not me!

If by chance you cross paths with me, Mr. Horsefly, on a wet-weather stroll, you have nothing to worry about: I'm a peaceful nectar sucker. But if you come upon my wife, watch out. She's the one who stings, bites, and cuts your skin with her knifelike **mandibles.** She even sucks your blood!

Easy for a lazy husband to say!

But don't think of her as nasty. Her bite is for a good cause. She needs blood for her eggs to grow. Mrs. Horsefly is an attentive and devoted mother.

The female horsefly, as our name suggests, is more likely to attack livestock than humans. We horseflies enjoy a quiet, shady spot on the prairie, where the fresh stream sings. (You didn't know we're poets, did you?!)

This country air feeds my poet soul...

Horsefly
(*Haematopota pluvialis*)
Tabanidae family
Diptera order
Insecta class

HOUSEFLIES

Yes, it's true—we **houseflies** really are annoying. And the more annoyed you get, the more you sweat, and the happier we are! What attracts us most in you humans is your moist skin. With our soft proboscis (that's a mouthpart used for sucking), we lick you and feast on your delicious sweat.

All this, of course, after being born in rotting garbage and stuffing ourselves with feces. We therefore carry lots of **microbes** (germs), which REALLY bugs you!

Housefly
(*Musca domestica*)
Muscidae family
Diptera order
Insecta class

All the methods you use to get rid of us won't do any good:

Flypaper, which will make one of us fall, all sticky, into your soup.

Insecticide, which stinks and suffocates you as much as it does us!

Or, clumsy as you are, the big **slap** that misses its target most of the time!

Do you know why you can't do anything to stop us? We overcome the shortness of our life (**17 days**—a fly's life is not very long) by producing a whole lot of offspring. A single fly lays about **150 eggs**...per day! That's one huge family.

Since a small sketch is better than a long speech, here's the story of our exciting lives:

Mommy, there's a maggot bugging me!

egg   larva (maggot)   pupa   adult insect   Whew!

Even though you hate us, we bet you can't help but admire our fantastic performances:

That pilot is such an ace!

ZZZ RRRROOOMMMM

Claw

Pulvilli (pad)

That's why we always put our feet in the plate.

We are very agile in the air. We have only one full-size pair of wings, but a second pair of underdeveloped wings called **halteres** (HALL-terz) help us stay stable and balanced in flight.

We have **sticky feet,** which allow us to walk upside down.

We can even taste with our feet because we have **taste buds** there.

Houseflies are the most common flies, but
you've probably also met some of our cousins.

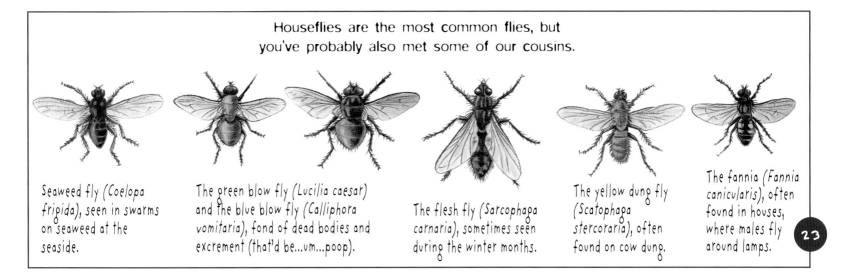

Seaweed fly (*Coelopa frigida*), seen in swarms on seaweed at the seaside.

The green blow fly (*Lucilia caesar*) and the blue blow fly (*Calliphora vomitaria*), fond of dead bodies and excrement (that'd be...um...poop).

The flesh fly (*Sarcophaga carnaria*), sometimes seen during the winter months.

The yellow dung fly (*Scatophaga stercoraria*), often found on cow dung.

The fannia (*Fannia canicularis*), often found in houses, where males fly around lamps.

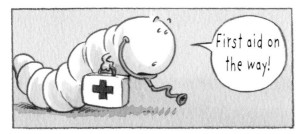

First aid on the way!

The **maggots** of one type of fly (*Phaenicia sericata*) can be used to clean wounds. The larvae eat the decomposing flesh while producing a substance that fights germs.

So you see, we can sometimes be useful. Without wanting to be a **gadfly** (busybody) or a **fly-by-night** (untrustworthy), I suggest that you don't **fly off the handle.**

Hey!

Watch it!

What's bugging you?

MOSQUITOES

WE MAKE YOU ITCH

Not many humans like us. Not only do we keep you from sleeping by buzzing in your ears, but we're also **hematophagous**—we feed on blood.

As with horseflies, only female mosquitoes bite, and for the same reason: so the eggs can grow. Mr. and Mrs. Mosquito don't look alike. Males have long feathery antennae and a proboscis that can't bite.

A mosquito bite doesn't hurt, but you'll soon be itching and scratching.

House mosquito
(*Culex pipiens*)
Culicidae family
Diptera order
Insecta class

Strutting around all day with his feather hat!

I know...

Just like my husband.

PSSSST! See how handsome I look?

They have nothing better to do!

Gilles
(*Homo sapiens*)
Bonotaux family
Primates order
Mammalia class

Larvae

Pupa

Maybe you've noticed that there are more of us near marshes, ponds, and pools. Stagnant water is our nursery—we lay our eggs there, and they hatch into **larvae.** Each larva then develops into a **pupa.** This picture shows how our young float just below the water's surface. They breathe with the help of a snorkel-like tube called a siphon that reaches the air. Each pupa develops into an adult.

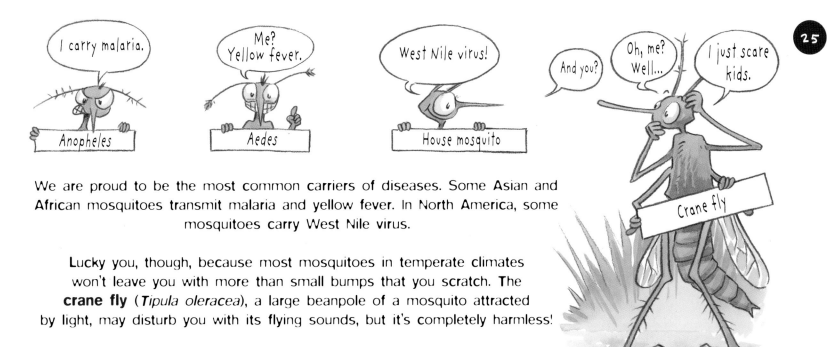

I carry malaria.

Me? Yellow fever.

West Nile virus!

And you?

Oh, me? Well...

I just scare kids.

Anopheles

Aedes

House mosquito

Crane fly

We are proud to be the most common carriers of diseases. Some Asian and African mosquitoes transmit malaria and yellow fever. In North America, some mosquitoes carry West Nile virus.

Lucky you, though, because most mosquitoes in temperate climates won't leave you with more than small bumps that you scratch. The **crane fly** (*Tipula oleracea*), a large beanpole of a mosquito attracted by light, may disturb you with its flying sounds, but it's completely harmless!

FLEAS

WE BITE

Take a close look. Aren't we **fleas** beautiful with our cute, round body and our legs designed for the long jump?

Did you know that even though we are only 3 millimeters (0.12 in) tall, we can jump to a height of 20 centimeters (7.8 in) and a distance of 40 centimeters (15.75 in)? That doesn't sound like much, but if we were your height, we could easily jump over the Notre Dame Cathedral in Paris. Amazing, huh?

And hop!

Human flea
(*Pulex irritans*)
Pulicidae family
Siphonaptera order
Insecta class

Hey, Drac, we share the same values!

What you surely appreciate less is the fact that we bite you and suck your blood. Adult fleas, both male and female, are exclusively **hematophagous.** Blood is our only food.

The creatures we live on are called hosts. But unlike a host that invites you to dinner, our hosts don't usually welcome our presence. Some of us live on dogs, others on cats, and still others on humans.

You are NOT welcome!

1 Mother flea lays about 100 eggs during her life. The larvae, which are like little worms, live on the ground and feed on debris.

2 Each larva then builds a cocoon in which it turns into an adult. This stage is called the **pupa.**

3 When we're big enough, we patiently wait for a host to pass by.

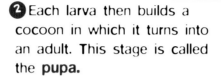

1,2,3...GO!

4 We can go for 40 days without eating, but when a host happens to show up, we jump at the chance!

Hundreds of years ago, during the Middle Ages, our ancestors carried a deadly disease called bubonic plague. The diseased fleas lived on rats, and rats lived in close quarters with people, and people spread it to each other. But humans don't need to fear us anymore. It's easy to keep us away—just keep yourself clean!

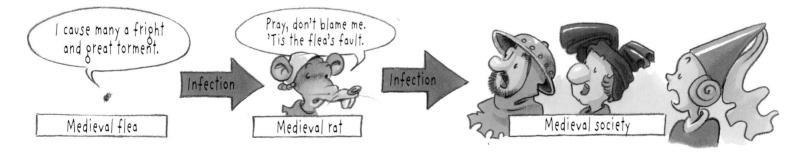

I cause many a fright and great torment.

Medieval flea

Infection

Pray, don't blame me. 'Tis the flea's fault.

Medieval rat

Infection

Medieval society

LICE

28

Lousy is another word for bad. You **call** someone you don't like a **louse** (or worse: a dirty louse!), a picky person is a **nit-picker**...What's next? It sounds as if you want to pick a fight. But we're simply doing what we were born to do: live on our host.

Unlike fleas, we **lice** remain faithful, living on our host's body all our life (scientists call that **ectoparasitic**). We cling to your hair and bite your skin. While our saliva keeps your blood flowing, we suck your blood. We lay eggs called nits that stick to your hair, and our children will follow in our footsteps—unless you get rid of us first.

Head louse
(Pediculus humanus capitis)
Pediculidae family
Phthiraptera order
Insecta class

I'm a louse. Can you get that straight?

We remind you,
with your cute little heads
(which we love very much),
that the plural of louse is lice,
just as mouse becomes mice,
but the plural of house is not hice
and the singular of ice
is certainly not ouse!

And together we're *lice!*

When your grandparents were young, the only way to get rid of us was to shave the heads of all lousy children. In those days, people used to call lice "cooties."

We move from host to host only by accident—when you humans put your heads close together, or you share combs or pillows. Nowadays, you have several easier ways of getting rid of us. We don't like **shampoos** or fine-tooth combs. You have **sprays** that poison us and **lotions** that kill us and our babies.

Careful, though. What doesn't kill us makes us stronger. We adapt, or change over several generations, until we become resistant to those products. Then they no longer work.

Despite what many people think, lice like clean hair as much as dirty hair. So it's not very bright to say that someone is dirty just because he or she has lice, or to feel ashamed because you've hosted us. We believe that everyone is equal, and that includes everyone—even school principals.

Yeah, that's right: **head lice** have no power against a bald guy.

Phew!

But there are other types of lice that bother human beings: **body lice.** These more readily attack adults, since children don't have body hair that lice can cling to.

This is annoying!

Shoot!

Thought I had nothing to worry about.

A little hygiene is enough to keep us away.

Oh really?

Great!

I'M SI-I-I-NGING IN THE... SHOWER

During times of war and famine, when people have more trouble keeping clean, body lice can become carriers of a terrible disease called **typhus.**

Like fleas, we lice are often unwelcome guests. And head lice and body lice (the most common types) are not alone. More than **6,000 species** of lice "invite themselves" to live with many hosts, both hairy and feathered. For animals from the walrus to the warbler, the bear to the weasel, we are the most annoying **parasite.**

Only the kangaroo doesn't attract lice. No one really knows why.

Some birds are so annoyed by lice that they settle down on anthills. The ants eat the lice and the bird feels better. Everyone is happy—except us, that is.

TICKS

We ticks are well aware that humans get "ticked" off by our blood-sucking habits. And after Thanksgiving dinner, we know you pat your gut and remark that you're "full as a tick." Well sorry if our thirst for the red stuff upsets you, but a tick's gotta eat! (You don't see us asking you to give up pizza, do you?)

Mother Tick lays her eggs in the ground. After hatching as larvae, young ticks enter the **nymph** stage, followed by adulthood. Perched at the tip of a tall grass blade or on a bush, we lie in wait to attack.

Tick
(Ixodes ricinus)
Ixodidae family
Acarina order
Arachnida subclass
Chelicerata class

Any mammal suits us, even you humans, though you're more likely to encounter us on your dog. We cling to skin, bite, and stuff ourselves with blood. We then become so fat that it's quite easy to spot us.

Author's note:
Don't tell the ticks this (they might be mad at me),
but I advise you to look for them in your dog's fur before they get fat with blood,
especially after a walk in the woods or tall grass. Seize this chance to
cuddle your canine friend (who will love it) while freeing him from
these nasty bugs, which can cause serious diseases.

1. Spot the tick! They are easier to see when they're full of blood.

2. Grab the tick's head with a tweezers.

3. Make sure to **remove** the head, not just the body. Return to number one and repeat!

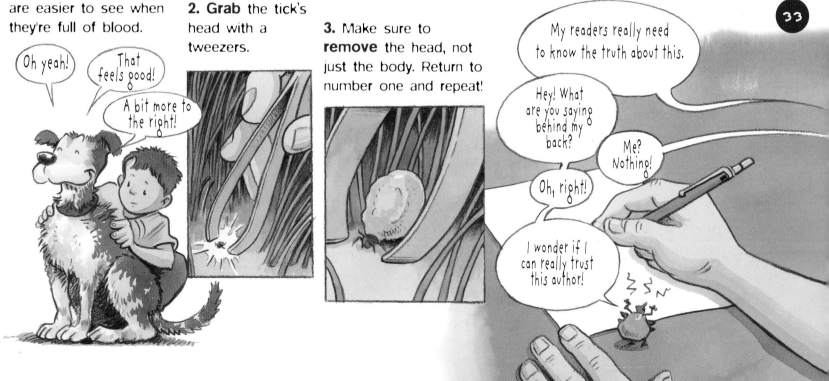

STINKBUGS

WE STINK

YUCK!

That's right, **stinkbugs** stink...and for good reason: so that no one eats us! When a bird is looking for an insect to eat, it would rather choose a fat grasshopper or a delicate moth to stuff its beak. That's because we stinkbugs are true to our name: a despicable, stinky, unappetizing lot, and proud of it!

When we feel threatened, we make a smelly substance that discourages predators from eating us. We sloe bugs are fans of berries, and you may have smelled us—or worse, crunched on one of us!—when you raided the berry patch.

34

BLECH!

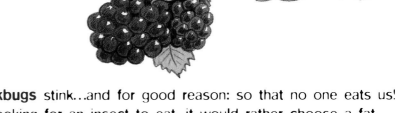

Oh my, these humans!

Not very smart!

There are more than 200 species of stinkbugs in North America alone. Many of them have colorful markings on shield-shaped bodies. Besides the bad smell, you humans have nothing to fear from us. We're **phytophagous** (plant-eating) creatures. We feed only on plant sap.

Sloe bug
(*Dolycoris baccarum*)
Pentatomidae family
Heteroptera suborder
Hemiptera order
Insecta class

The water measurer and the water strider glide on the water's surface like skaters

Stinkbugs are part of a larger group that you humans call "true bugs." Now, we're not sure what that means for the other bugs in this book...I mean, are they fakers? Anyway, scientists have an even more fancy name for members of this group: Heteropterans (part of the Heteroptera suborder).

These insects are found all over the world. Some Heteropterans spend their lives in and around water. All the aquatic species are **predators,** which means that they hunt and eat other animals.

the water scorpion (*Nepa rubra*)

the water boatman (*Corixa punctata*)

the biting water bug (*Naucoris cimicoides*)— Watch out for its painful bite!

the backswimmer (*Notonectidae*)

BEDBUGS

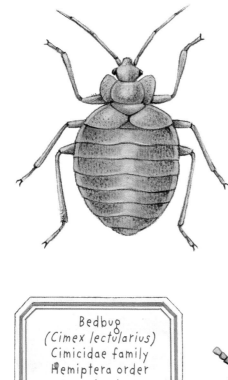

We **bedbugs** can brag about being as bothersome as our buddies, fleas and lice. Like them, we are **parasites** (we live at the expense of our host) and are hematophagous. (Oh no, please don't ask me what that means. We've already explained. Listen, if you keep this up, there will be a test at the end of the book. And that's that!)

We are tiny and completely flat, which allows us to cling to your skin at night and bite you. We hide in **cracks** or in mattresses during the day.

Bedbug
(Cimex lectularius)
Cimicidae family
Hemiptera order
Insecta class

Like fleas and body lice, we often thrive during times of misery, poverty, and war.

General Louse, you will attack from the north while Sergeant Flea will launch an assault from the east.

Victory is ours!

We've known humans for a long time. At the dawn of civilization, when your ancestors lived in caves, our only hosts were the bats and birds that lived in the same shelters. Later we got used to you and grew to love your blood.

In French, the word for bedbug (*punaise*) also means "thumbtack."

Like fleas, we can go without food for a long time, but if that happens, we won't get any bigger. After each meal of blood, we **molt:** this means that we shed our skin for a bigger one. Many insects grow like this.

SPIDERS

WE ARE SCARY

Ahhhhhhh!

Hey, what's the matter?

I haven't done anything.

For some humans, it seems there's nothing more terrifying than a spider...but why? Is it our overall appearance you find repulsive, or just our hairy legs? Or is it that we lurk in the high corners of your houses, watching everything you do?

I'm the tegenaria, the **house spider,** the one you drown in your bathtub without pity, the one you squash with a look of disgust. But please believe me—I'm totally **harmless** to humans, as are most spiders!

I wouldn't even hurt a fly!

Oh yeah? Says who?

38

House spider
(Tegenaria domestica)
Araneae order
Arachnida subclass
Chelicerata class

We spiders can be identified not only by our physical characteristics, but also by the form of our webs.
Are you smart enough to match up each of us spiders with the correct web?

We spiders aren't cruel. We only hunt to feed ourselves. And we must point out that some of our **hunting techniques** are pretty awesome!

Hunting scene on the web.

| The web moves... | The spider moves toward its prey... | wraps it... | injects the venom... | and enjoys. |

Some spiders don't have webs, so they hunt by lying in wait or by jumping on their prey. Even spiders that don't build webs spin silk threads, which they use to wrap their prey, to make egg sacs (small nests for the baby spiders), to move around, and even to fly!

When some young spiders emerge from their sacs, they climb a tree, stick their abdomen in the air, and spin a long thread. The thread acts as a "dragline," so that the slightest breeze carries them very far. This is called **parachuting.**

Parachuting spiders can go as high as 3 to 4 kilometers (1.5 to 2.5 miles), and as far as 100 kilometers (60 miles). After this performance (that is, if they survive—these trips can be dangerous) the little spiders will manage very well on their own.

Our mating techniques are a bit complicated. Male spiders are often smaller than females, so Mr. Spider has to be a gentleman if he doesn't want to be wolfed down by an annoyed female.

Mr. **Thomisid** silently approaches his mate, ties her up, then quickly runs away after mating.

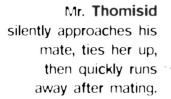

Mr. **Pisaurid** captures a fly, which he wraps in silk and gives to his mate. If she accepts it, then he is allowed to mate with her.

Mr. **Lycosid** and Mr. **Salticid** charm the ladies by dancing. (They are much more elegant than the rude Mr. Thomisid.)

Several spiders, including Mr. **Epeira**, use females' webs to send signals to them first—much like a phone call or an e-mail.

CONCLUSION

After listening to each of us, we hope you understand that the organisms you carelessly call "bugs" are in fact a marvelous mix of insects, arachnids, and chelicerates that swarm, wriggle, and breed at your feet. And while you are able to kill a lot of us with your **pesticides** and **insecticides,** future generations of bugs will survive these, becoming even more resistant.

What's more, you run the risk of destroying species that are useful to you and upsetting the fragile **ecological balance** of our blue planet. Think about it—like **all** living things, don't we deserve your respect?

Who doesn't eat?

Who takes more than his share?

Who eats whom?

Who isn't alive to eat anymore?

Who eats what?

Enough questions... Let's eat!

OK...One last thing. Did you know that there's another meaning of the word *bug?* At the beginning of the computer age, cockroaches made their way into some of your giant antique computers and caused big electrical problems. Nowadays, there are nasty programs that can get into your computer and destroy stuff you have stored there. We call these programs "computer bugs." And they are one class of bugs that it's OK to hate!

And don't think we're done with you yet!

43

TEST!

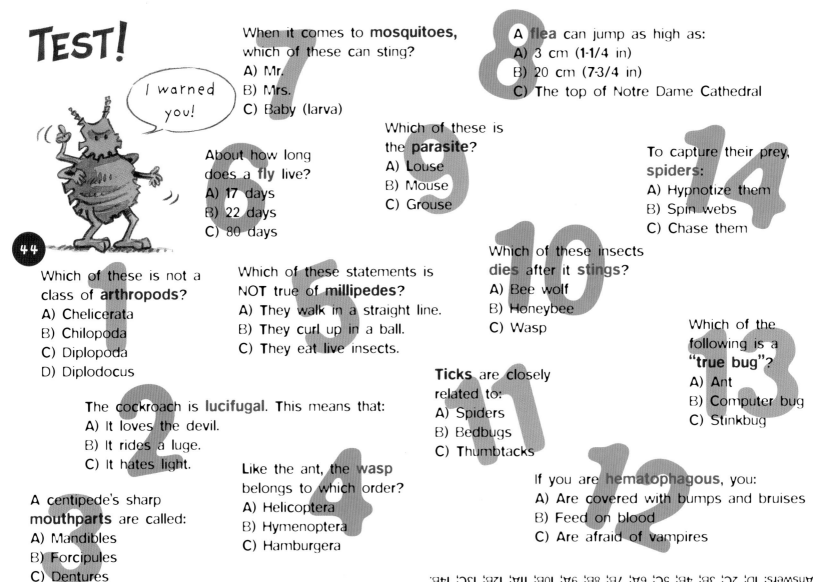

"I warned you!"

44

7 When it comes to **mosquitoes**, which of these can sting?
A) Mr.
B) Mrs.
C) Baby (larva)

8 A **flea** can jump as high as:
A) 3 cm (1-1/4 in)
B) 20 cm (7-3/4 in)
C) The top of Notre Dame Cathedral

6 About how long does a **fly** live?
A) 17 days
B) 22 days
C) 80 days

9 Which of these is the **parasite**?
A) Louse
B) Mouse
C) Grouse

14 To capture their prey, **spiders**:
A) Hypnotize them
B) Spin webs
C) Chase them

1 Which of these is not a class of **arthropods**?
A) Chelicerata
B) Chilopoda
C) Diplopoda
D) Diplodocus

5 Which of these statements is NOT true of **millipedes**?
A) They walk in a straight line.
B) They curl up in a ball.
C) They eat live insects.

10 Which of these insects **dies** after it **stings**?
A) Bee wolf
B) Honeybee
C) Wasp

13 Which of the following is a **"true bug"**?
A) Ant
B) Computer bug
C) Stinkbug

2 The cockroach is **lucifugal**. This means that:
A) It loves the devil.
B) It rides a luge.
C) It hates light.

11 **Ticks** are closely related to:
A) Spiders
B) Bedbugs
C) Thumbtacks

3 A centipede's sharp **mouthparts** are called:
A) Mandibles
B) Forcipules
C) Dentures

4 Like the ant, the **wasp** belongs to which order?
A) Helicoptera
B) Hymenoptera
C) Hamburgera

12 If you are **hematophagous**, you:
A) Are covered with bumps and bruises
B) Feed on blood
C) Are afraid of vampires

Answers: 1D; 2C; 3B; 4B; 5C; 6A; 7B; 8B; 9A; 10B; 11A; 12B; 13C; 14B.

WORDS TO KNOW

abdomen: the bottom section of an insect's body

antennae: the long, thin feelers on an insect's head, used for tasting and touching

apterous: lacking wings

arthropod: any member of the Arthropoda phylum, which has jointed legs and a hard skin called an exoskeleton. Crustaceans, spiders, insects, centipedes, and millipedes are all arthropods.

carnivore: a meat-eater

exoskeleton: a hard covering that gives shape and support to an arthropod's body

hematophagous: feeding on blood

host: an animal whose body provides food and shelter for another animal

larvae: the wormlike young that hatch from the eggs of some insects

nymphs: the young of some kinds of insects, which look like small versions of their parents

omnivore: an eater of meat and plants

parasite: an animal that lives and feeds in or on the body of another animal

phytophagous: feeding on plants

pupa: the cocoon stage of some insects' lives, between larva and adulthood

saprophagous: feeding on decaying matter

thorax: the middle section of an insect's body, where the legs and wings attach

BUG INDEX

45